This copy of Lost in the Snow
belongs to:

Along with the author and
illustrator, field mice: Rachel, Jack and Uncle
Olivier, hope you enjoy reading the story.

Michael R Beddard   Rebecca Yoxall

ACKNOWLEDGEMENTS

Very many people have helped with the creation of this book. I am very grateful to them all and, especially, to my dear friend Caroline Cliffe; to my amazingly supportive sister, Pam Beddard; to my mother, Edith Beddard; to 'Percy', the field mouse who started it all; Tony Coll; The Players Theatre, Davenham, and to Vanessa Duffy and the children of class 2 at Norley Primary School.
MRB

NO MICE WERE INJURED IN THE MAKING OF THIS STORY

First published in Great Britain by Michael R Beddard, June 2012,
Northwich, Cheshire, CW9 8DA.

http://beautybankpublishing.blogspot.co.uk

For online orders:

www.TalesfromBeautyBank.etsy.com

ISBN 978 0 9573022 0 4

beautybankpublishing@gmail.com

Tales from Beauty Bank

LOST IN THE SNOW

by
Michael R. Beddard

Illustrated
by
Rebecca Yoxall

DEDICATION

For my father, Jack Beddard.

Story originally written for my god daughter
Rachel Louise Tomlinson.

Introduction

During my 33 years as a teacher, I saw at first-hand how very important it is to educational success to get children interested in books from an early age. I also saw that the vital spark for this interest often comes from adults reading stories to, or with, children or when different generations are able to talk about stories they have both enjoyed.

Lost in the Snow is an enchanting example of the type of book which gathers together all ages. Its places, personalities and events speak just as vividly to an older generation as to the very young. A pleasure to read-aloud, or to enjoy independently. And with twists and illustrations that will delight and warm the hearts of children and grown-ups alike.

As a long-time resident of Cheshire, I also like that this story, as with the rest of the **Tales from Beauty Bank** series, is set in the county. The story doesn't reveal the exact location of Beauty Bank, but it really does exist. What's more, the little village theatre is real, too. And once upon a wintry day, the theatre had some unexpected visitors. So what happened then? Read on. Find out.

Caroline Cliffe

"An island Farm, mid seas of corn, Swayed by the wandering breath of morn. The happy spot where I was born"

Lewis Carroll

The snow was falling quite fast now; Mrs Walker made her way over to the window to close the curtains for the night. As she did so she noticed the large snowflakes floating down like little umbrellas from the night sky. Mr Walker was sitting in front of the coal fire finishing his cup of tea and stroking their pet cat Peggy, who was enjoying the warmth and attention.

The clock in the hallway struck six. Mr Walker was the caretaker of the theatre in the village of Beauty Bank and it was his job to open up the theatre each night for rehearsals and performances and to operate the lighting and sound equipment for plays.

"Well, Peggy," said Mr Walker, "it's no use me sitting here. I shall have to wrap up and set off for the theatre".

Mrs Walker brought in Mr Walker's hat and coat, scarf and gloves. "Oh, thank you, dear," said Mr Walker, "I had better set off a little earlier tonight. If that snow decides to stick, it will delay me getting to the theatre on time". He put on his warm clothing, and picked up his keys from the hall table. "Well, I'm off then, dear. See you later."

As he opened the front door, the light from within the room lit up the snow on the pathway outside. As far as the eye could see was white over - just like a large white blanket.

Turning to shut the door, he noticed little Peggy peeping out at the snowy scene, too. But the cat, knowing she was in the warmest place, made no attempt to venture out with him into the snow-filled night.

His journey to the village theatre was short. The snow was already quite deep in parts and made a crunching sound with every step. Soon Mr Walker arrived at the theatre building. He pulled off his gloves and put them into his pocket, pushed the key into the lock of the door and with a firm turn of the handle opened the door wide.

Reaching inside, he flicked on a light switch, giving the theatre a warm welcoming glow. Then, not wanting to tread in the wet snow, Mr Walker stamped his feet on the doormat.

Moments later he was indoors with the door shut behind him - unaware of the little visitors who had scurried in with him from the cold.

They were now huddled together on the first step of the theatre's staircase: three little mice - Uncle Olivier, Rachel and Jack.The youngest mice had been out exploring the village of Beauty Bank with their uncle when the snowstorm started. There was no chance of them making it back to Uncle Olivier's house by the river; the snow was up to their little armpits. Uncle Olivier said their only hope was to find some other shelter for the night.

It was a stroke of luck, then, that Rachel noticed the lights come on in the theatre and the open door as Mr Walker shook the snow from his boots.

Mr Walker made his way into the kitchen to turn on the heating system. Meanwhile Rachel, Jack, and Uncle Olivier started out on their big adventure. Uncle Olivier beckoned to Rachel and Jack to follow him up the stairs.

He maintained that his great grandfather's motto was "when in doubt or in danger, go onwards or upwards", so Rachel and Jack, who could not at that moment think of a reason for not agreeing with Uncle Olivier, followed without delay. It was quite a climb, and at the top step they were greeted by two doors, both firmly shut.

The one on the right had a piece of wood missing a little way up and to one side, just big enough to allow a small mouse through. Jack said he thought he could possibly reach the hole by standing on his tiptoes. "Very well," said Uncle Olivier. "Onwards or upwards."

Jack made a jump for the hole and managed to squeeze through. After a quick check for danger, he gave Rachel the word it was safe to follow.

Now it was Uncle Olivier's turn. He managed to grasp the hole in the door but, being rather tubby around the waist, needed some help. Jack and Rachel held one arm each and on the count of three, pulled Uncle Olivier through the hole and down onto the floor in a heap.

The light from a street lamp opposite the window cast an orange glow into the room and as their little eyes became accustomed to the light, they found themselves in the theatre's costume room.

Rachel's eyes opened wide when she saw the wonderful clothes all around. Dresses that sparkled, hats with feathers, shoes and boots in every colour. Jack squealed "I could be a soldier, a cowboy, or even a fireman", while, Uncle Olivier explored the rim of an old top hat.

Snowstorms, strange places, climbing and exploring are all very tiring, though. So they were ready for a rest by the time Uncle Olivier found a large hatbox lying on its side and suggested they hide away in it and sleep.

As the little mice drifted off, Rachel dreamed she was a beautiful princess with lots of wonderful dresses; Jack was a brave knight in armour slaying a bad dragon, and Uncle Olivier was.. well.. just asleep.

The next morning, the distant, yet familiar sound of the church bells brought Uncle Olivier out of his deep slumber. Rachel and Jack slowly left their dreams behind them and so began another day.

Jack scurried up the curtains and onto the window ledge to look out at the street below. He noticed that a small pane of glass was missing. Carefully, Jack popped his head out of the window and felt his little nose tingle in the cold frosty air. The snow had stopped falling now and Jack looked around admiring the view.

To the left he could see the village church with its tall steeple climbing high into the sky, and the last few people arriving for church. The bells gave a final peal before fading out into silence.

To the right, a large oak tree, its branches like long fingers, reached out over the road, almost touching the window ledge. Beyond the tree was a clear view of the road leading through the village. Apart from the two people walking along the snow-covered pavement towards the theatre, the village was peaceful.

Jack was rather cold by now and decided to return through the broken window to find Rachel and Uncle Olivier. He was just about to climb back into the hatbox, when, a loud bang startled him. Rachel and Uncle Olivier jumped out of the hatbox, calling, "Jack, Jack, where are you?" "Here, Uncle Olivier!, I'm all right. The bang was the door downstairs."

The mice listened carefully.

At the hole in the door, Rachel could hear two people talking: a man and a woman. After a few minutes footsteps on the staircase sent Rachel, Jack, and Uncle Olivier rushing back into the hatbox. There, the little mice heard the chattering sound of the door latch and the creak of the door opening.

Hardly daring to breathe, they peeped out and saw an elderly lady. "Now where did I put those clothes for mending," she said, looking around the room. "Oh, here they are". As she walked to a table piled high with costumes, she caught the hatbox with her shoe - causing the box to shake and the little mice to fall over and roll around inside.

Rachel scrambled back onto her feet, just in time to see the lady with her arms full of clothes going out of the room, leaving the door wide open.

Uncle Olivier volunteered to go through the open door first - rather relieved that this time he would be spared the embarrassment of a huff, a puff and a sharp pull.

Finding everywhere quiet, he beckoned to Rachel and Jack to follow. Out on the landing they noticed the door opposite was also open so peeped in. In one corner was a large mirror and in it a reflection of the most wonderful sight they had ever seen - a table heaped with the most splendid banquet: oranges, apples, and Jack's most favourite food of all, bananas.

Uncle Olivier and Jack scurried straight towards the table, using nearby books as steps, but Rachel paused to admire her reflection. She quite liked the idea of being a ballerina and so decided to practice dancing.

Jack was soon at the fruit bowl, looking hungrily at a shiny red apple. With one big bite he tried to sink his teeth in but made no impression at all. Puzzled, he next took a bite at a banana, with just as little success. This wasn't real fruit, it was plastic. Not a feast for a mouse at all.

Uncle Olivier stood by scratching his head, "Never mind, Jack". "Let's see what else we can find". "Onwards or upward my boy!"

When Uncle Olivier and Jack rejoined Rachel at the mirror, she was still dancing and now practising standing on her tiptoes. The sight was so entrancing that none of the trio noticed the black shadow closing over them. Suddenly, before they could run for cover, they were scooped up from the carpet in a soft felt trilby.

It was Mr Walker. In the hat he carried the mice down the stairs, across the stage and into the theatre's sound and lights room, where he set them safely down on top of an old sideboard, saying: "Don't be frightened, little friends.

"I know it is very cold outside. You are welcome to stay here until the weather warms up. Now then, I wonder if I can find you a little treat before the play rehearsal starts?"

Mr Walker went then to his coat which was hanging over the back of a chair in front of a bench full of lights, knobs, levers and switches. From his coat pocket he pulled a large foil-covered block which he unwrapped and placed in front of the three little mice. Chocolate!

But Rachel was far too interested in all the flashing lights and switches to think about food. She left Uncle Olivier and Jack tucking in while she watched Mr Walker setting the lights on the control board flashing or glowing in lots of different colours.

Best of all, she thought, was the big black switch that Mr Walker slid up and down, controlling all of the lights on the stage.

Lights fascinated Rachel. She had once stayed with a cousin who lived in a large department store in Manchester, and had fond memories of flicking all the switches on and off in the electrical room behind a curtain in the toy department.

Over the next two weeks the weather did not improve. The snow fell thick and fast and had turned into ice. The little mice found a large empty light-bulb box where they could snuggle together every night. The real thrill, though, was watching as the theatre company got ready to perform their play.

They especially liked how excitement grew backstage as the audience began to arrive; seeing Mr Walker set out the important instructions about when to turn the stage lights on or off and, most of all, the magic of the play itself.

Before long, the little mice felt as though they could walk out onto the stage and perform the play themselves.

On the morning of the last performance, the little mice awoke to the sound of the birds chattering on the guttering outside. Uncle Olivier broke up some rich tea biscuits that Mr Walker had left for them, and shared the pieces with Rachel and Jack.

"The birds are making a lot of noise this morning," said Uncle Olivier. "Have a look outside, Jack, and see what is going on." Jack scampered off but could still see nothing but snow and could hear only water dripping.

When he returned, Uncle Olivier asked: "Anything to report?". "Not really," said Jack. "Just a drip-drop dripping sound". "Dripping?" said Uncle Olivier. "Then, the snow and ice must be melting at last".

Rachel's face lit up at the thought of being able to return to Uncle Olivier's house by the river, but she felt a little sad too. She had enjoyed their stay in the theatre. "Still," she told the others, "at least we can watch the final night of the play before we go home."

As the day went on, the little mice hid away as different people called into the theatre to do various jobs: the wardrobe mistress to gather up clothes; the carpenter to adjust the stage set and cleaning ladies to vacuum and dust and by lunchtime, the theatre was quiet again.

Jack was having fun, running up and down the see-saw he had created by balancing a wooden ruler on a screwdriver left on the lighting room bench.

Rachel was sitting on the window ledge looking out on to the stage and trying to remember exactly what happened in the play - where the actors stood, the words they spoke, but most of all, the moment when Mr Walker operated the big black switch which illuminated all the wonderful coloured lamps, reminding her of rainbows and magical adventures seeking pots of gold on rainy days.

Uncle Olivier snoozed on.

Suddenly, a door downstairs banged loudly. Uncle Olivier woke with a start. "What's that? Who's there?" On his tiptoes, he squinted in the late afternoon gloom through the window on to the stage.

Just beyond the stage he spotted a dark shadowy shape carrying a long sharp-pointed stick. "Hide, children, hide!" Uncle Olivier called out.

Rachel and Jack scurried quickly into a corner; Uncle Olivier ducked behind a pile of books on the sideboard. Their little hearts were pounding hard as the footsteps became louder and louder, nearer and nearer.

Each mouse trembled as the door knob turned slowly, the door creaked ajar and the light flicked on. And that is when the mice saw.... kind Mr Walker, dressed this time in a hooded anorak and carrying a dripping umbrella.

Rachel sighed with relief when she recognised their friend while Uncle Olivier lay down on a book, his eyes closed, ready to return to sleep. Mr Walker hooked his damp coat around his chair then turned on a small fan heater to dry it, much to Uncle Olivier's warmth and delight.

Scariness gone, Rachel and Jack began exploring a shelf full of cables and spare light bulbs for the theatre lamps. Balancing on the bulbs was difficult for the little mice. Their little feet kept slipping and sliding on the shiny surface of the glass. Rachel giggled at Jack's wobbly walking across the bulbs and laughed almost until she cried when she saw the strange reflection of his face in the glass.

But her laughter turned to a gasp when Jack suddenly slid off a light bulb, off the shelf and clear out of sight.

Rachel hardly dared look. The shelf was high and she feared Jack must have hurt himself in his fall. Jack was shocked, to say the least, but seemed in one piece – just very unsure of where he had landed and in total darkness.

Using the balancing skills she had gained from her ballerina practising, Rachel picked her way across the light bulbs, looking here and there all the time for Jack. She reached Uncle Olivier at the sideboard. "Whatever is the matter?" said Uncle Olivier, seeing her anxious face. "It's Jack," said Rachel. "He fell off the shelf, and is lost, very lost."

Uncle Olivier pricked his ears. He could definitely hear a "Help! Help!" In fact, Jack was shouting so loud, it was a wonder Mr Walker couldn't hear him, too. Uncle Olivier's problem was - he just couldn't see Jack.

As Jack shouted louder and louder, Rachel and Uncle Olivier turned this way and that trying to locate where the cries were coming from. Making this more difficult, though, was that every now and then Mr Walker would whistle a tune or mutter aloud a comment about his switch settings.

Uncle Olivier and Rachel were quite at a loss as to Jack's whereabouts. Whilst the two mice searched high and low for Jack, Mr Walker suddenly realised that he had forgotten the important papers which gave him instructions when to operate the lights at the end of the play. "Oh dear", said Mr Walker. "I had better dash home and collect them. The audience will be arriving soon and if I'm quick I will just make it back in time." And with that, he scooped up his coat and went out.

Stuck in his dark prison, Jack was now very long-faced. He was tired of calling for help, and fearful that he would never see the light of day again. He was just about to call out to Rachel one more time, when something rather odd occurred.

The walls of his prison started to move, and he had the strangest feeling of being lifted upwards. As Jack looked up a thin beam of light shone down, allowing him to make out the soft white floor, and a chocolate bar wrapper. Jack soon realised he had fallen off the light bulb shelf and straight into Mr Walker's coat pocket!

Mr Walker fastened up his coat but paused before leaving to switch on a music player, to entertain the audience before the actors and actresses gave their final performance.

Though the music wasn't loud, it did prevent Rachel and Uncle Olivier from hearing Jack's new cries for attention.

So, as Mr Walker disappeared through the door, they were amazed to see Jack waving the corner of a white hankie from Mr Walker's coat pocket. Rachel and Uncle Olivier were beside themselves with worry. "Should we follow Mr Walker and attempt to rescue Jack?"

But older and wiser Uncle Olivier said no. "Mr Walker is coming back with his papers. We shall just have to pray he brings Jack back as well."

Mr Walker left the theatre door on the latch, in case any actors arrived while he was out, before hurrying towards home, quite unaware of his little travelling companion.

Jack soon got used to sitting inside the pocket and was excited to recognise the places he had seen when looking out. There was the village church and the oak tree with finger-like branches, and now he could also see people inside several of the cottages they passed. He wished more than once that Rachel was with him; they both so enjoyed adventures.

Mr Walker was in such a rush he could only spare a hasty 'Hello' when he met the village store-keeper Mrs Green, out with her dog Holly.

Even so, he knew he had to tread carefully; the thaw was making the pavement very slippery.

Mr Walker had just opened the gate to his house when disaster happened. In slushy snow, his feet shot from beneath him and he crashed to the ground with a bump.

Jack had a very narrow escape. If Mr Walker had fallen differently, Jack could easily have been squashed flat. Instead, he scrambled out of the coat pocket and saw poor Mr Walker lying on the path and groaning: "Oh, my back, my back!" Jack felt so sorry and helpless and so wished Rachel was with him; she was always full of good ideas. He stood, twisting his little whiskers and trying hard to think what Rachel would suggest if she was there.

Back at the theatre, the actors and actresses had arrived and were getting ready, unaware that Mr Walker was missing.

They saw the lights, heard the music and assumed he was in his lighting room as usual. When the audience turned up, too, and began taking their seats, Rachel and Uncle Olivier started to worry even more. "Mr Walker should be back by now," fretted Rachel. "Where is he? And where is Jack?"

Jack, meanwhile, was looking down the path towards Mr Walker's house. Its curtains were partly open and the light shining through the little square windows was casting large square patterns on to the snow outside.

The light also cast the shadow of what looked to Jack like a huge great monster – in fact, it was Mr Walker's cat, Peggy, peering through the glass.

Jack was tempted to run from the beastly shadow but he also wanted very much to help poor injured Mr Walker. It was then that he noticed a rose trellis next to the window and remembered Uncle Olivier's advice: "When in doubt, or in danger, go onwards or upwards".

"That's it!" thought Jack. "Upwards! And I sure hope that glass is strong.

Breathing hard, Jack climbed the rose trellis and crossed on to the slippery cold windowsill, reminding himself once more that there was a sturdy piece of glass between him and the monster. Then with the deepest of breaths, the little mouse started marching back and forth along the ledge, right under the cat's gaze.

As soon as Peggy spotted Jack uproar began. She lashed out, flashing her sharp claws across the window and hissing loudly through bared teeth.

The fuss brought Mrs Walker rushing to see what the all the commotion was about. And through the window she saw poor Mr Walker, now sitting upright on the ground but still moaning and rubbing his back.

Jack knew he couldn't hang around until Mrs Walker opened the door and helped her husband to his feet; Peggy the monster was unlikely to miss the chance of a mouse-flavoured supper! So, muttering 'Onwards', he began scurrying back towards the theatre as fast as his little legs could carry him.

As Jack approached the theatre, the church clock pealed out the passing of time. The street was busier now, with people arriving to watch the play. He had to dodge between large feet to reach the entrance. One boot came so close to treading on him, Jack could see his own scared face reflected in the shiny shoe leather.

It was a relief to stand on the doormat leading into the theatre, to warm his chilled toes and catch his breath before climbing the stairs that led to the lighting room.

In the room, Rachel and Uncle Olivier were at the window overlooking the stage. Row by row, the theatre was filling up with people. Uncle Olivier scratched his head. "Mr Walker is cutting it more than a bit fine, Rachel. What can have happened to make him so late?"

A loud "clunk" startled the two mice. They both looked over towards the music player Mr Walker had left running. The music had come to an end; the machine had switched itself off.

Rachel's eyes opened wide as she remembered the play she had been watching ever since Mr Walker had brought them to this room. The first actor was now centre stage. "Oh no!" she said. "The play has started without Mr Walker. Whatever shall we do, Uncle Olivier?"

Uncle Olivier paced up and down the windowsill with his hands clenched behind his back, and a worried look upon his face. "Something is seriously wrong, Rachel. Mr Walker - and Jack - should have returned by now." A single tear ran down Rachel's cheek. She turned away from Uncle Olivier and looked out onto the stage, her vision blurred.

Just then a sound from the corner of the room attracted her attention. It was Jack, squeezing his way through the gap in the lighting room door. "Oh Jack! Jack!" cried Rachel. "Uncle Olivier, its Jack!", "Jack! My dear boy", "what a relief," cried Uncle Olivier. "I've been worrying my ears off. Where on earth have you been?"

Jack positioned himself with his back to the fan heater, wiggled his little bottom as the warm air slowly took away the chill.

"Well," said Jack, "we went through the village and saw lots of houses, and shops, and people, and dogs, and…" "But where is Mr Walker?" asked Uncle Olivier.

"Well...", said Jack again, "we went flying on the slushy pavement and we turned upside down and I climbed up really high and fought off a huge great monster with claws, and.....

"Jack," said Uncle Olivier sternly. "This isn't the right time for your tall stories, I'll ask again - where is Mr Walker?" "Oh, him. He isn't coming," said Jack. "Mr Walker hurt his back when he fell down in the slush."

Rachel covered her face with both hands, "Whatever shall we do now? No Mr Walker, no important papers, no pretty coloured lighting effects. Whatever shall we do?"

At this, they all stood in silence, staring out onto the stage. They could just make out what the actors and actresses were saying. It was then that Rachel had one of her wonderful ideas. "There might just be an answer".

I've been watching Mr Walker all week. I think all the switches are in the right places. The only one that needs operating is that big black one. Mr Walker slides it just as the lady in the blue dress leaves the stage near to the end of the play."

"Rachel. We're mice. How do you think we'd ever be able to work a big switch like that?" said Uncle Olivier. They all peered down at the big black switch. "Look where it is," said Uncle Olivier. "How would we even get down to it, let alone move it?"

Rachel looked around the room and her eyes came to rest on the wooden ruler that Jack had used earlier as a see-saw. "I've got it. If we can wedge the end of Jack's see-saw in this slot, we'll have a springboard...."

"And.......?" said Uncle Olivier, clearly very puzzled.

"And with you weighting it down at that end, Jack and I can leap onto the switch and push it down. But we need to work very quickly; there isn't much time." When the ruler was in place, she beckoned for Jack to join her. "I can't," he said. "I'm so tired, and I think I've done enough bouncing about and jumping for one day, if you don't mind."

"Well, actually I do mind," replied Rachel. "Mr Walker helped us and now we must help him. Just pretend you are a pirate walking the plank".

On the stage, the final scene was in progress.

Uncle Olivier gave Rachel the thumbs up as the lady in blue left the stage. At his signal, Rachel gave reluctant Jack a big shove and soon after both were up in the air heading towards the control switch and shouting: "Onwards, upwards!"

Thud one. Jack landed first and felt the switch shift ever so slightly beneath him. Thud two, Rachel added her weight and grinned as the big black switch began to slide slowly but steadily forwards.

Then, all at once, the whole stage was illuminated with the most spectacular display of coloured lights making Uncle Olivier dance up and down so excitedly calling: "Bravo!" Bravo!" that he tipped himself off the ruler.

In the hall, the audience was also cheering and clapping. "Oh, children," said Uncle Olivier. "What a splendid job. You've saved the day and I am sure Mr Walker would be very proud of you".

Jack yawned. "That was fun but, please, can we go back to the river now. I can hardly keep my eyes open and I want my own bed." "Okay, sleepy-head," said Rachel, turning to take one last glance at the pretty twinkling lights with a quiet smile, "let's go home".

As they got outside the theatre, Uncle Olivier shivered; it was still chilly and he could see his breath in the evening air. The snow was melting quickly now, and as the mice ran towards the road they could see lumps of snow sliding down the rooftops and dropping onto the street with a "thump".

At the road, a large black car pulled into the kerb, its big headlights shining so brightly in the darkness that for a moment Jack thought it was an owl swooping down to drag him away.

The driver got out and went to help his passenger to get out. It was Mr Walker! He limped slowly towards the entrance, just in time to meet one of the actors on his way out. "Jolly good lighting again, Mr Walker. Your timing is always spot on. Well done".

Mr Walker paused at the theatre's door with a puzzled look upon his face. He'd come to say sorry for letting the players down, so why was he being thanked.

He was still shaking his head in disbelief when his eye was drawn to a fresh patch of snow which had fallen from the roof of the theatre.

Written in the snow in tiny footprints were the words:

"Thank You"

Mr Walker turned and looked towards the church, with its very tall steeple climbing high into the night sky, and in the golden glow of the street lamps, he could see three little figures, wending their way homewards.

THE END